ASTRID the Fly

Maria Jönsson

Holiday House / New York

And this is my sofa.

I can walk on the ceiling,

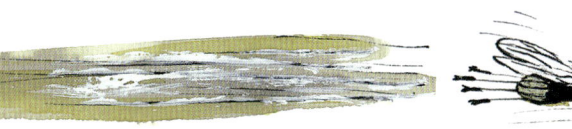
fly superfast,

I have big eyes,

2 arms,
    2 wings,
        and 4 legs.

and do daredevil nosedives.

I live behind the sofa with my family:
Mom and Dad, Grandpa and Grandma,
Aunt Ally,

7 cousins,
3 second cousins,
and 43 brothers and sisters.

Sometimes I have to take care of the baby flies. But I'd rather go exploring.

After that I like to see what's happening behind the **warm window**.

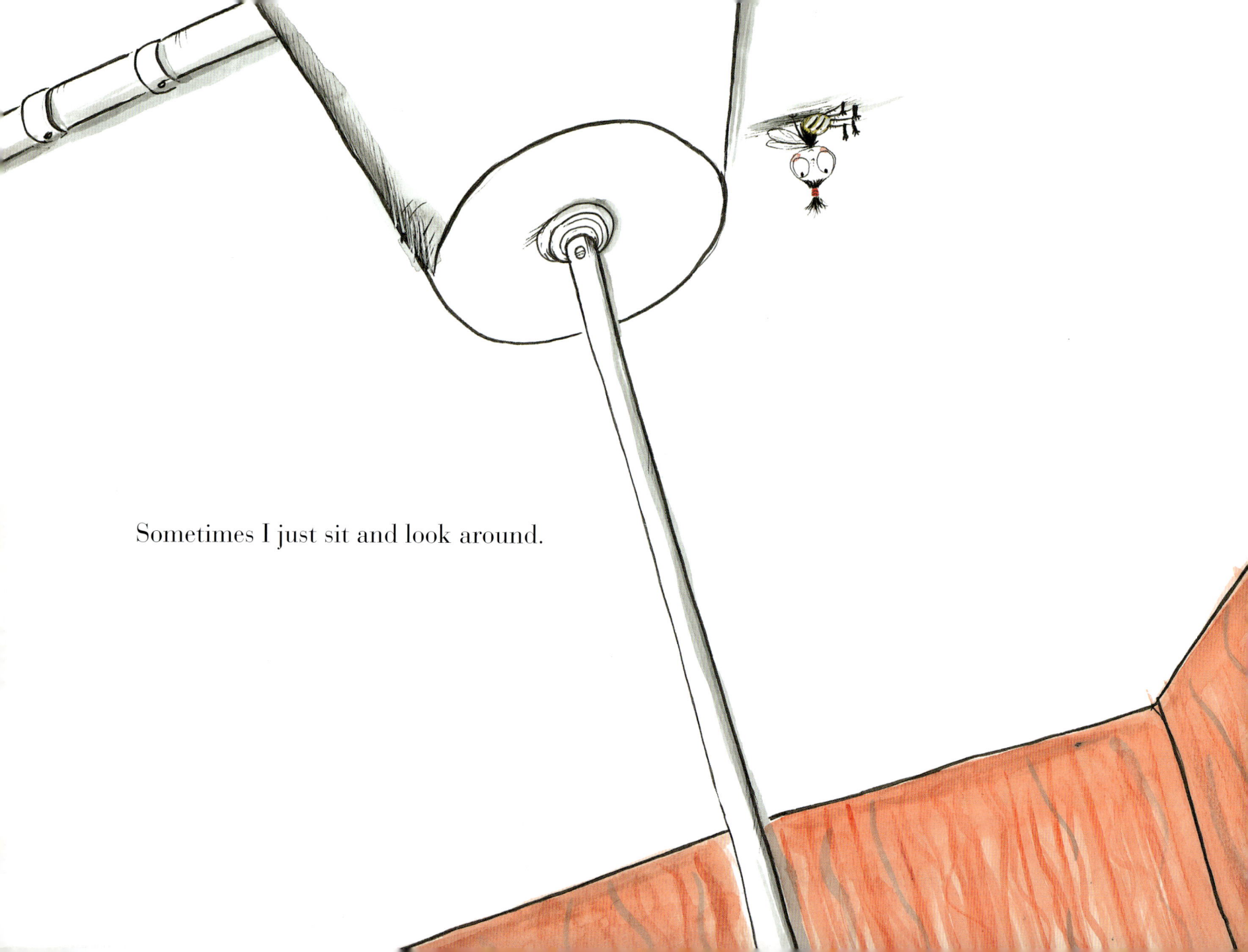

Sometimes I just sit and look around.

Or I go to the see-me glass and say hello to myself.
"Hi, gorgeous!"

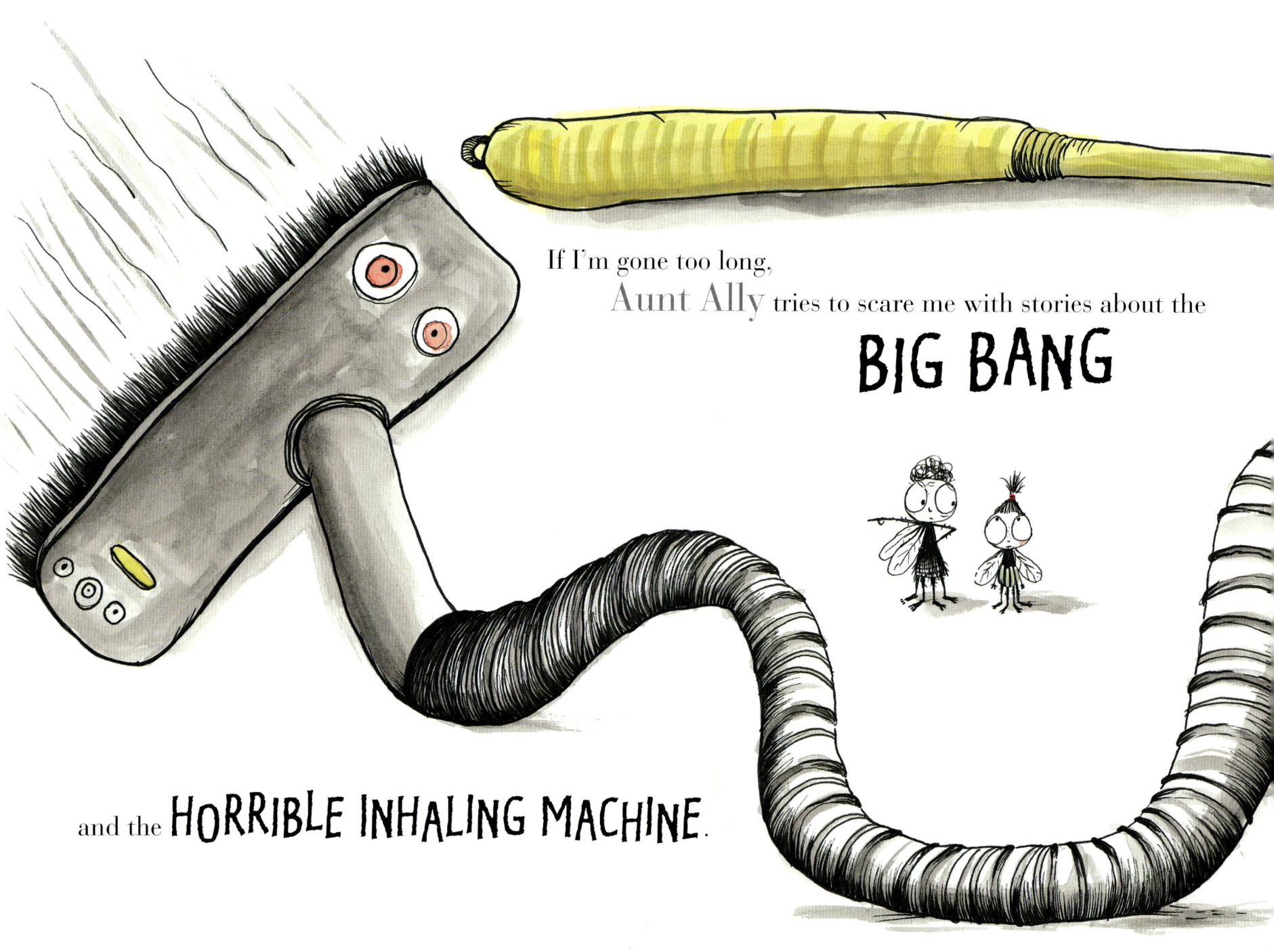

If I'm gone too long, Aunt Ally tries to scare me with stories about the BIG BANG and the HORRIBLE INHALING MACHINE.

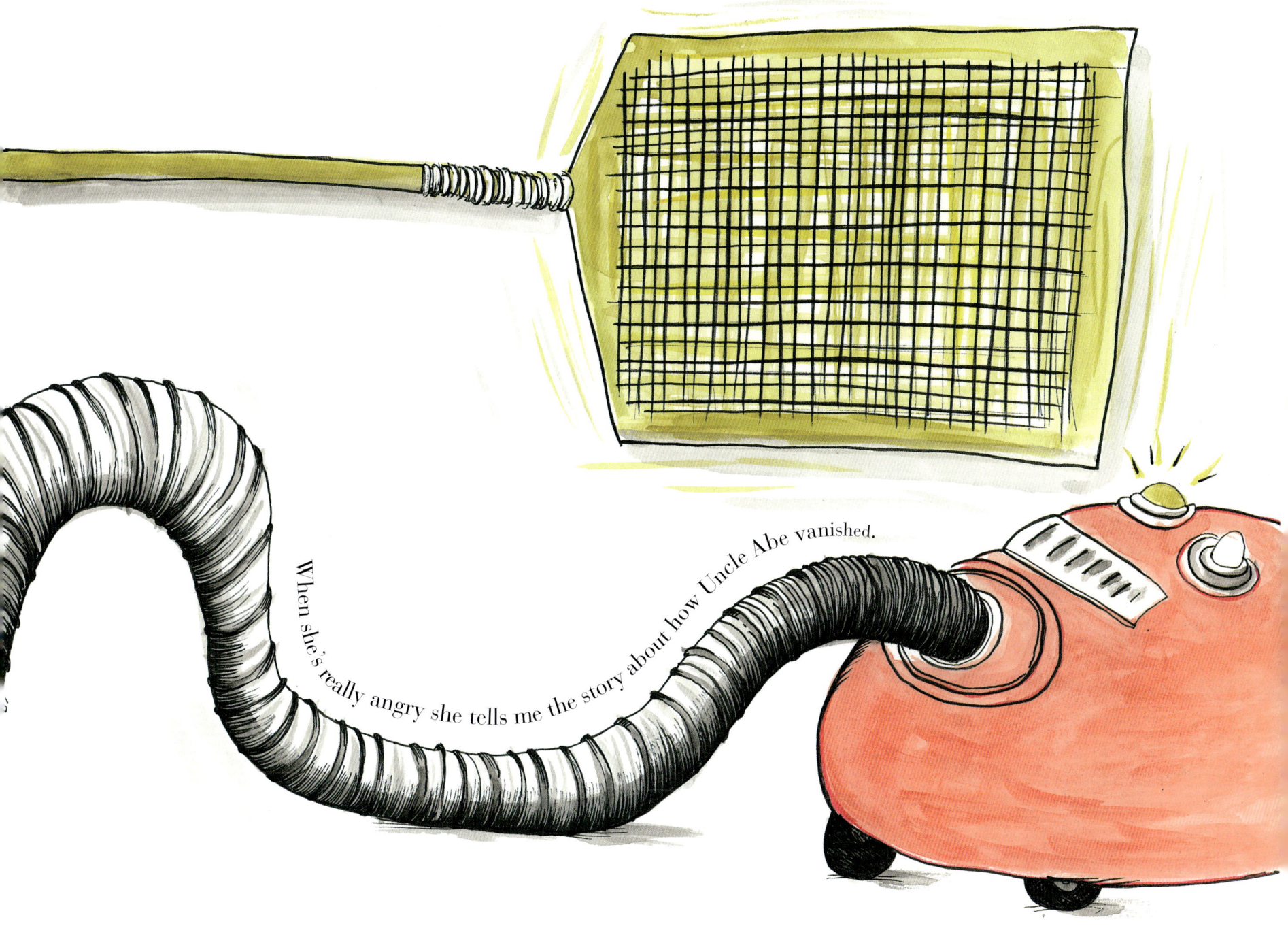

Sometimes I fly at night, when it is safe. At night I don't have to worry about the BIG BANG and the HORRIBLE INHALING MACHINE or how Uncle Abe vanished.

But during the day there is FOOD.
And I like food.
I like . . .

1. soft brown things

2. sweet wet things

3. red sticky things

4. and white small things.

But my favorite is
DANISH SALAMI.

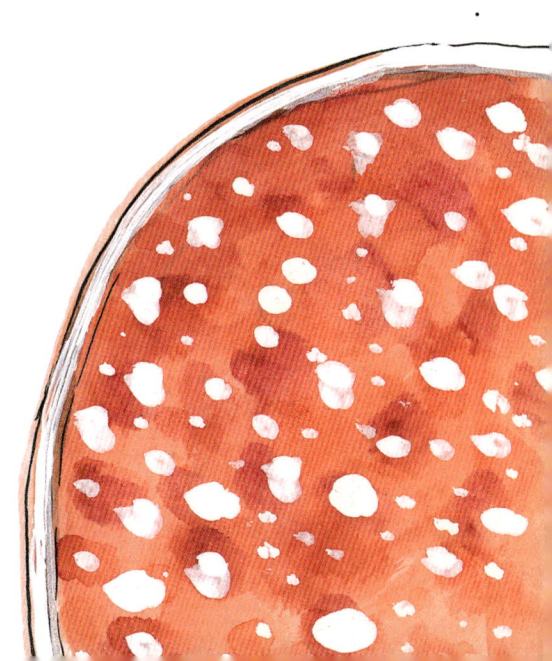

I LOVE
Danish salami.

Once I ate so much that I fell asleep.

And I didn't know what was happening to me.

When I woke, it was dark and cold . . .
so cold I couldn't move my wings.

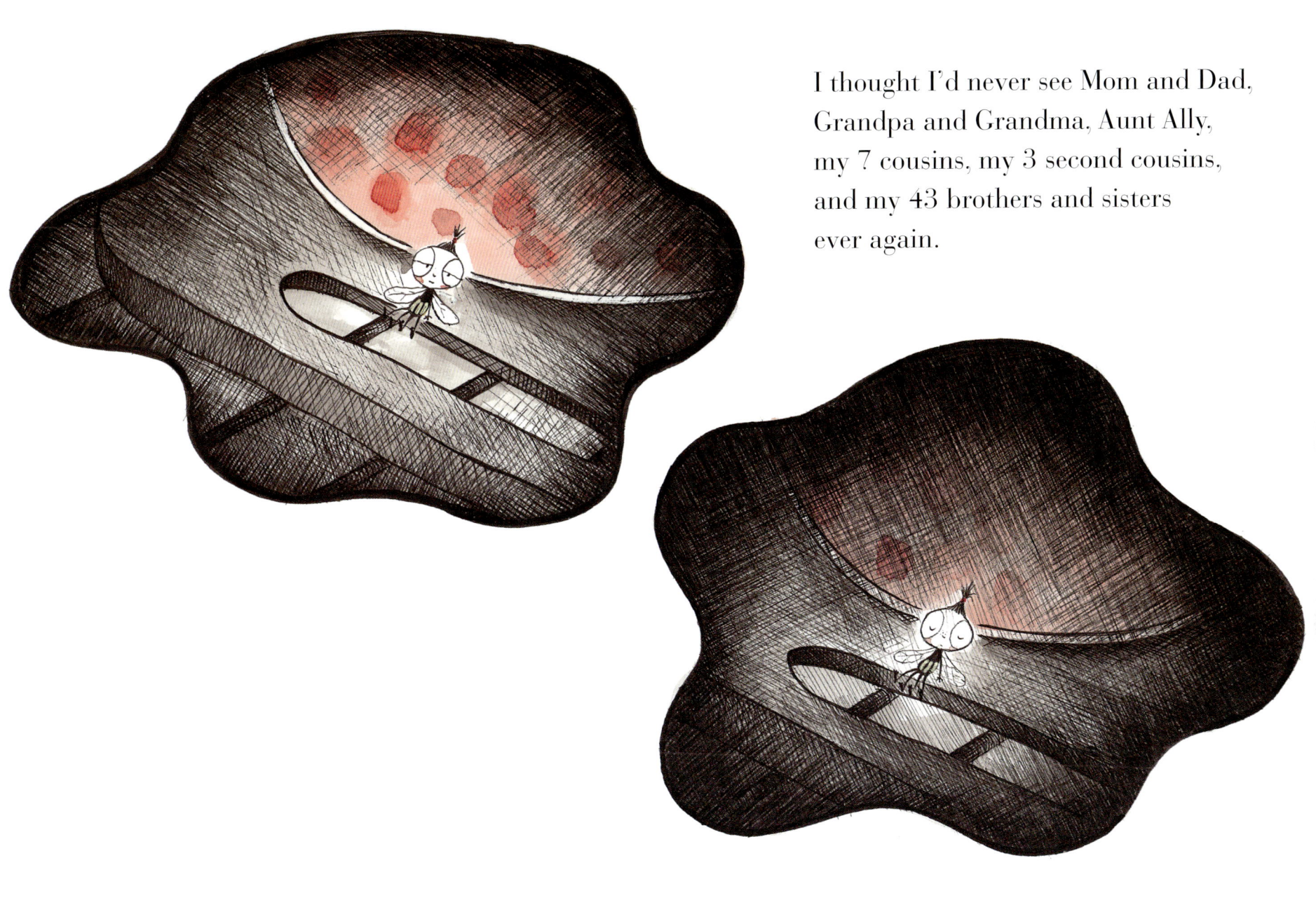

I thought I'd never see Mom and Dad, Grandpa and Grandma, Aunt Ally, my 7 cousins, my 3 second cousins, and my 43 brothers and sisters ever again.

Suddenly, everything became **light**.

As I dried my wings by the warm flat black sun, I thought,

"I'll never eat Danish salami again!"

When I got home to the sofa, Mom needed my help with the baby flies. And Aunt Ally had been looking for me.

Of course, Aunt Ally was angry. But she was so glad to see me that she didn't even ask where I'd been. That was a good thing, because I didn't know where I'd been.

And since that day, I eat only green things.